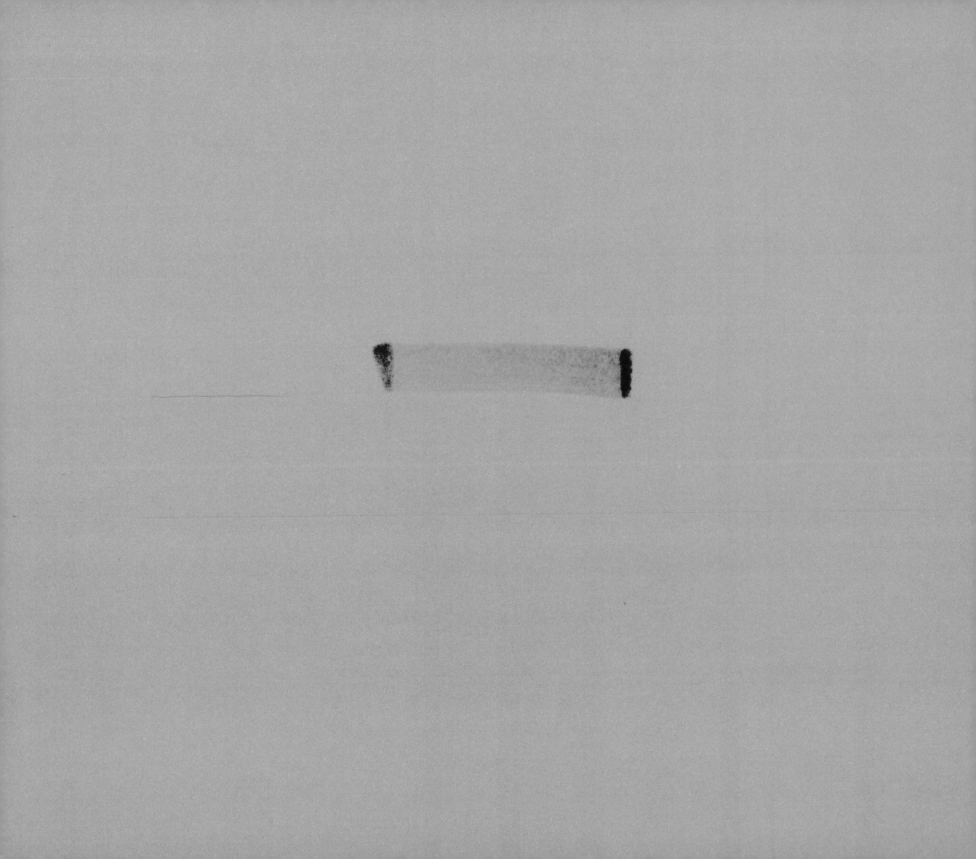

ALICE YAZZIE'S YEAR

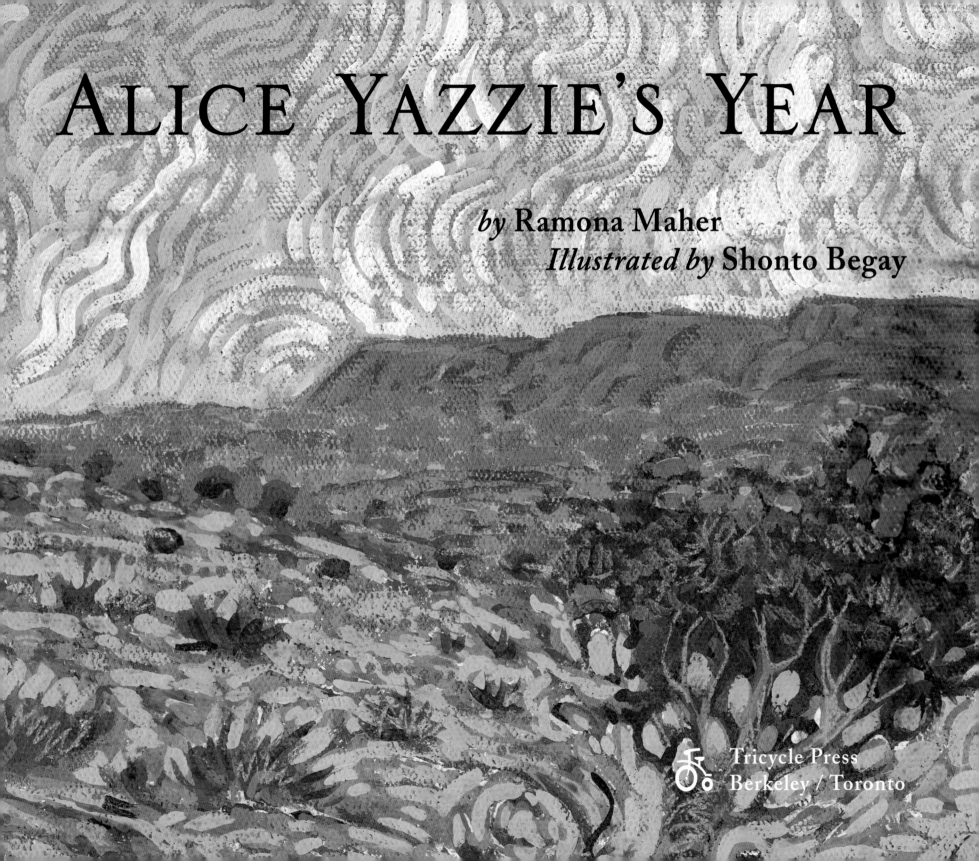

ALICE YAZZIE'S YEAR

by Ramona Maher

Illustrated by Shonto Begay

Tricycle Press
Berkeley / Toronto

January ■ YAS NIŁT'EES

The snow slowed the world,
the Navajo world.
"Go see if the sheep are fine,"
Grandfather Tsosie tells Alice Yazzie.
"The hay is frozen
and so is the ground," says Alice, returning.
"The horses look like they blame me
for causing this cold."

Her nose red, her chin buried in sheepskin,
she carries the smallest lamb
into the hogan.
"Just for the night," says Alice Yazzie
holding the lamb.
"He's all new and starry.
He's too new to be cold."
Grandfather grunts.
He doesn't say no.

Alice heats milk in a bottle
over burning pinyon.
Grandfather watches.
The new lamb sucks.
The pinyon burns low.
The lamb goes to sleep.
His nose is a black star.

"It *is* cold out there," Alice tells Grandfather
as she goes to bed.
Grandfather nods.
He wears a red flannel shirt Alice gave him for Christmas.
He looks at the low fire.
He looks at the lamb.
Grandfather says
to Alice Yazzie,
to Alice Ben Yazzie,
"It was almost this cold
the night you were born."

February ■ ATSÁ BIYÁÁZH

Alice Yazzie waits in the snow
for the yellow bus.
Yellow bus takes kids to school,
to the picture shows,
to the doctor for shots,
past the black earth
strip mined for power—
the kind of power
that white people know.

It hums through big wires
across Black Mountain,
across red canyons.
It isn't the power that Grandfather knows,
thinks Alice Ben Yazzie.
White Shell Woman told him soon they will leave:
the men and earth movers.
"Rainbows will come back," Grandfather says.
"Blue Corn Woman promises we shall have the land back.
All this will be ours."

The bus is late.
Alice watches the poles and transformers,
the big caterpillars grinding the earth.
Will they leave too late, wonders Alice Yazzie.
Will Grandfather travel to the spirit world
with the snow all dirty?
Will Dawn Boy find him?
Will the world grow clear?

March ■ WÓÓZHCH'ÍÍD

Alice Yazzie is going to see
Mickey Mouse, Donald Duck, Tinker Bell, and Snow White.

She's off to Disneyland, Los Angeles, San Francisco.
Will a mouse tuck her to sleep
on a goatskin blanket?
Will a smoke hole let cooking smoke
out of the hogan?

Alice Yazzie doesn't believe—
but she wants to go.
(Do Disney elephants truly have pink ears?
Say hello?)
There are places
one simply has to go
given the chance.

Grandfather Tsosie watches her leave
on the yellow bus.
"I will see you later," he says.
She's back in six days.
Grandfather smiles.
"Back so soon, Alice Yazzie?
Tell me all that you saw."

"I saw Evonne Goolagong hit a million tennis balls.
I saw stores with Levi's all sewn with flowers.
I rode a cable car.
I saw a machine making chocolate. A machine that made ice.
I saw Alcatraz. I saw Mickey Mouse."

She takes a deep breath.
"I missed frybread," says Alice Yazzie.
"And I missed you, Grandfather.
The worst thing was: nobody listened.
The nicest thing was coming back here."

April ■ T'ÁÁCHIL

Jimmy Benally had a pet coyote
with yellow eyes.
Nobody else wanted it.
It grew up to be
a long, gold shadow—
no more yellow pup.
He took off one day.
"That's just the way
them coyotes do," said Mr. Benally.

"He had to go," said Jimmy to Alice.
"He's smart, that fellow.
He can tell his shadow
from all of the others.
He was my coyote,
a different fellow.
He can hide and then smile.
He's out there teasing rabbits,
walking on his blue feet."

Alice Yazzie knows that Jimmy Benally
watches for shadows, listens to howls,
wonders about pawprints in the sand.
"He'll never come back.
He just grew up," said Jimmy Benally,
"and he had to go."

May ■ T'Ą́Ą́TSOH

Alice Yazzie rides her horse
in the barrel racing
at the rodeo.
She pays twenty-five cents
to see a buffalo
with a mangy coat
in a small cage in back of a trailer.

He is a buffalo out of Montana.
He has humped shoulders
and slits for eyes.
They look red from smoke
like a drunk bronc rider's.

After hamburgers and ice cream on a stick,
Alice leaves the crowd, the squash blossom auction,
the men judging baskets,
and goes back to the cage.

The buffalo snorts.
He hoofs at the ground.
"Don't be so loud," Alice tells him, drawing closer.
He eats six lumps of sugar
out of her purse.
He nibbles the turquoise
on her left hand.

"Is blue your color?" laughs Alice Ben Yazzie,
a nugget in her throat too big to swallow.
"Just remember, old blossom eater,
you can stare down the wind.
This old rodeo
Ain't everything."

June YA'IISHJÁÁSHCHILÍ

Jimmy Benally
got hit by a truck
and is in the hospital.
"Tuba City doctors," prays Alice,
"please fix up Jimmy."

Alice finds a yellow pup
with a coyote father.
"Get up, Jimmy, please get up,"
she says outside his window
to the tubes, through the glass,
holding up the hazel-eyed puppy
so Jimmy can see its footpads are blue.

The doctor with the stethoscope
shakes his head, no.
Alice wonders, though,
whether Jimmy saw the puppy
before he died.

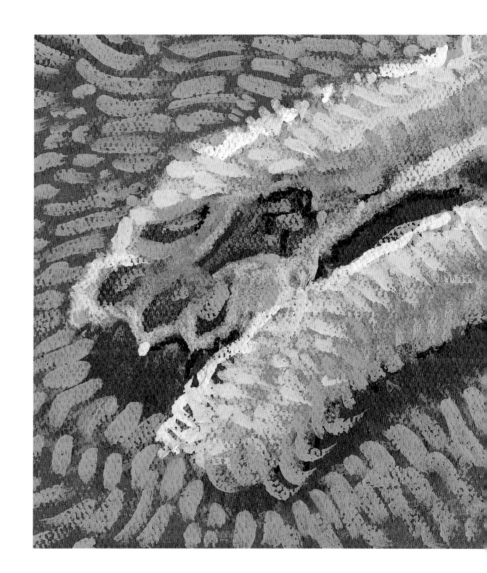

Nobody wants the yellow pup,
so Alice keeps it.
She calls the dog Jimmy.
It has yellow eyes and a black nose.
It has ears that perk up
at the smallest sound.
It is her friend
and is named for a friend.

July ■ Ya'iishyáástsoh

Clouds boil like icing
on store-bought cupcakes.
Alice likes coconut.
Grandfather likes chocolate.
Alice goes marketing,
wearing blue velvet.
Jimmy, her pup, is a sun dog behind her
as she walks three miles to the trading post
and three miles back.

"Six miles for cupcakes
and strawberry pop!" says Grandfather proudly.
"And dark roast coffee,"
Alice reminds him.

Alice knows you drink coffee
when you grow up.
She likes coffee a little,
with milk and with sugar.
(Bertha Begay pretends
to like it a lot.)

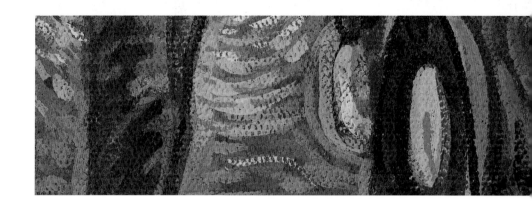

August ■ Bini'anit'ą́ą́ts'ózí

Alice Yazzie has new brown shoes
and a white dress.
The preacher's wife
drives her to Sunday School.
That's all right.
Then there is church.

Alice listens, then leaves
during Hymn 97.
She walks five miles to the hogan.
She's already home
when Mrs. Johnson drives up.
"You'd get tired, too," says Alice,
tucking her shirt into Levi's,
"if you were eleven
and had other things to do."

Mrs. Johnson's upset.
Alice is sorry.
"I did like the song about leaning,
leaning on the longest lasting arms,"
says Alice, shining the dusty brown shoes.

"Another time, then."
Mrs. Johnson smiles.
"Another time, Alice."

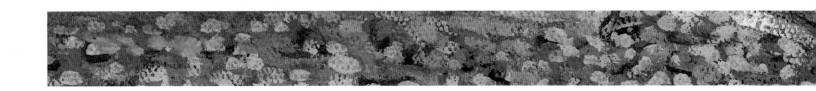

September ■ BINI'ANIT'ÁÁTSOH

Alice pulls her hair back in one long braid.
Last year's gym shorts are too short. She's grown.
Her toes won't even wiggle
in last year's tennies.
It's a mile through the dust
to the yellow bus stop. In winter: through mud.
The pup seems to beg with his eyes:
"Stay home. Let's us play, Alice Yazzie.
The two of us."

Grandfather frowns.
"We do what we must.
I see you must go to school. This year—
not so many hot dogs in the cafeteria.
More books in the learning center.
We'll see to that."
Grandfather sits on the school board
and helps decide about classes and buildings.
The oldest school board man, he sees change happening.
He says it must come.
He even voted for girls to play football
if they want to. And study computer drafting.

Alice starts off in her tie-dyed T-shirt
and a denim skirt faded canyon blue.
Grandfather calls. He gives Alice a ride
behind him, on his horse,
to the bus stop shelter.
Alice is surprised.
"Remember," says Grandfather,
nudging the old mare until she faces around.
"You don't have to take computer drafting
if you don't want to."

"Thank you, Grandfather."
As they move off, old man on old horse,
Alice feels winter coming.

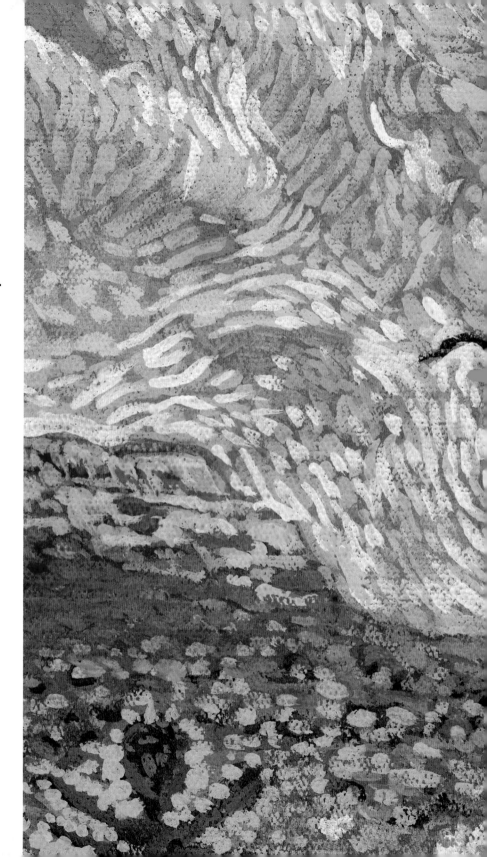

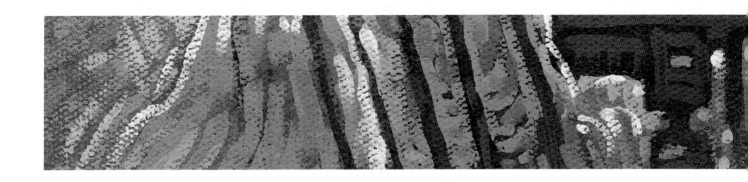

October ■ GHAAJI'

All the second graders are cutting up pumpkins.
The third graders are stringing the seeds.
The school cafeteria has served pumpkin pie
most of the month.

Among other things, Alice
is learning to sew. She's going to make
a Hallowe'en costume for the school carnival
like no one else's.
The pleats will be hard.
Tom Singer is a red pitchfork devil.
Bertha Begay will go as a pirate.
Alice won't tell what her costume is.
She learns about facings.
She rips pleats out twice from the white sharkskin.
Square necks are hard.
"If this thing had sleeves,
I'd never finish," mutters Alice, staying in recesses,
whipping and stitching.

On Hallowe'en evening,
she hands Grandfather some Mickey Mouse ears—
his Hallowe'en present.
He laughs and laughs.
Jimmy barks and barks.

Grandfather fastens the ears
over Jimmy's crisp ears.
Alice laughs to see that.
Grandfather likes Jimmy
a little bit, maybe.
"And who are you?" asks Grandfather. He stares
at the cardboard tennis racquet.
"Aren't your legs bare?"
Alice sees him thinking about new ways.
Computer drafting.
"I'm Evonne Goolagong. Champion tennis player.
I come from the billabong! I can wear this next spring
on the new tennis courts!"

"Evonne Goolagong," Grandfather says.
"Evonne Goolagong. I like that name."
They eat some licorice and wait for their ride.
"Billabong," Grandfather marvels
under his breath.

November ■ NÍŁCH'ITS'ÓSÍ

"The Pilgrims never landed here," Alice Yazzie tells the teacher,
"but we had quail and turkey and pheasant
before the white men killed them.
We still have squash and corn."

That day,
Alice makes up a song called
"We'd be glad to see Columbus sail away."
She sings it during study hall.
She sings it for Mr. Takesgun when she gets sent
to the principal's office.
Mr. Takesgun is a Kiowa from Oklahoma.
He smiles a little at Alice's song.

"Well, Columbus got lost, you know," he said.
"Somebody had to find him,
so we did the job."

Alice goes back to class, smiling,
imagining Indian canoes bumping the *Santa Maria*
and the pop-eyed captain claiming for Spain
what never was lost in the first place.

"He was sad we weren't peppercorns.
He hoped we'd be cloves," thinks Alice,
making up new words for the song.

December ■ NÍŁCHʼITSOH

The baby's name was Immanuel
and he had small shoes.
He knew about lambs—cold ones without mothers.
He knew that the way to understand is to listen
to stars and to buffalo, to stones, and to water.

Alice Yazzie knows the stable stood
someplace in a desert, where minute by minute,
the burro carried Mary closer to straw and a nearly full inn.
"I'll weave a rug," thinks Alice Yazzie,
picking burrs from some wool.
"I'll card and I'll spin.
When the snow is deep, the light will shine from it.
Time is the thing," thinks Alice Yazzie.
"Next spring, next shearing—I'll have enough wool."

Alice's grandmother's beautiful rug hangs on the wall,
the wall of the hogan nearest her bed.
The white square in the center means the world in a storm.
The gray squares in each corner
are the homes of the clouds.
Clouds bring rain from the sky.

Rain drives spiders indoors.
Red and yellow flowers open and the desert turns green.
Lightning bolts are four zig-zag lines
that streak out from their homes:
from the four places of clouds to Mother Earth.
Water bugs sit between clouds, waiting for rain.

Alice sleeps in a house safe from storms.
The water bugs woven snug in the rug
are her friends by night. They watch in the mornings
when Alice wakes up.
"All of my life, no harm can get me," thinks Alice.
She watches the rug when lightning lashes her mountain:
ghosts chasing their tails.

"My grandmother's rug brings soft rain to the desert,"
Alice writes in a theme.
"We still have the rug.
We still have Grandmother's loom.
Next year, Mrs. Manygoats will teach me to weave.
Beauty is before me.
Beauty is around me."

"Grandmother, am I your beautiful girl?"
asks Alice Yazzie, looking into a mirror.
"May next year bring beauty around and before me.
I am safe here."

Jimmy yips, chasing a dream.
Grandfather's tobacco is under the tree,
wrapped in bright paper.
Grandfather snores.
He's made her a bracelet, she's almost sure.
Blue and silver—the way the world is.

Silver snow lies on Black Mountain, hiding the gouges.
The sky is blue in daytime,
leading, guiding
her back to the beginning.
All the beginnings, thinks Alice Yazzie,
age twelve next week
and beginning to see,
beginning to feel.

Notes about the Navajo country and ways of life

Alice Yazzie's Year, by Ramona Maher, is a wonderful month-to-month story about a Navajo girl. I would like to make a little commentary on each month from January to December, and also a few other notes about our culture.

Navajos call JANUARY "Yas Niłt'ees," which means crusted snow. It gets real cold in January, and when you walk on frozen snow you can hear it crunch under your feet. In Navajo, "yas" means snow and "niłt'ees" could also mean roast or cook, but today most Navajos say "Yas Niłt'ees" means crusted snow. Our language is so old that, probably, in the early days when the Navajo language was limited, it could have meant boiling or thawing snow for water.

FEBRUARY is called "Atsá Biyáázh," which means little eagle, or eaglet. In our country, February is the month when eaglets are hatched.

MARCH is called "Wóózhch'ííd," which means the cries that young eagles make.

Navajos call APRIL "T'ą́ą́chil," which means the reawakening of plant life in the spring after the winter sleep.

MAY, in Navajo, is called "T'ą́ą́tsoh," which means the growth of plant life.

JUNE has a long name in the Navajo language— "Ya'iishją́ą́shchilí"—which means the planting of early crops.

JULY also has a long name—"Ya'iishyáástsoh"—which means the planting of late crops.

AUGUST also has a long name—"Bini'anit'ą́ą́ts'ozi"— which means, in Navajo, the maturing of early crops.

SEPTEMBER is called "Bini'anit'ą́ą́tsoh," the maturing of late crops.

Navajos call OCTOBER "Ghąąjı̨'." This means the dividing of the seasons. Winter starts in October and lasts through March, and from April to September is considered to be summer.

NOVEMBER is called "Niłch'its'ósí," a mild, cold wind.

DECEMBER is called "Niłch'itsoh," a big cold wind— and it gets cold in December as well as in January.

Now let's go back to January, Yas Niłt'ees, and learn a little something about some of the things mentioned in the story that you may like to know more about.

Alice's name, Yazzie, is a word that, in Navajo, means little or tiny. Her grandfather's name, Tsosie, in Navajo, means slim. These names are heard a lot in Navajoland.

Navajos raise sheep, and children frequently herd them. They raise sheep for wool and they sell their lambs in the fall for money. They shear their sheep in the springtime when the weather gets warm and some of the wool they sell and some they save to weave beautiful Navajo rugs like the one that Alice's grandmother wove. Navajos also raise goats and cattle. The sheep and cattle are sometimes sold for their meat. Lamb is the Navajos' favorite meat.

Alice lives in a place called Black Mountain, Dzilijiin. The mountain is associated with Blessingway rite traditions as a sacred mountain. White Shell Woman and Blue Corn Woman, who are mentioned by Grandfather, are Holy Women in our religious stories.

He also mentions Rainbows. Rainbows are regarded as protection and are considered as guardians protecting plants, mountains, and clouds. Whenever you see one in a Navajo sandpainting, which is a religious picture, you know that it means protection.

Dawn Boy is the symbol of dawn, which is East. Horizontal Skyblue Boy is the symbol of South; Yellow Evening Twilight Boy is the symbol of West; and Black Darkness Boy is North.

Many Navajo children go to schools run by the United States government, known as Indian schools. Many of them are boarding schools. Sometimes they will sponsor a trip for students and take them to places away from the Navajo country where they can have fun and also see and learn something about how things are in the big cities and places away from the reservation.

Navajo children like to have dogs for pets. Coyotes though are not usually considered for pets. There are many stories about Coyote. Most of the stories about Coyote picture him as a trickster. When he does tricky things, he always ends up the loser. He is the symbol of greed, wantoness, lust, envy—all the desires that can get him into trouble, sometimes even ending his life. This may be why no one else wanted Jimmy Benally's coyote pup. Coyote did help the Holy Ones long ago, even if he was a bit tricky about it, and when he associates with Them everything comes out alright.

Rodeos are a must in places all over the Navajo country. They are very popular from spring through summer and when school is out, some of the older students take part. Young girls are really good in barrel racing, which is riding your horse in a pattern around a number of barrels without knocking them over. Many Navajo men dress like cowboys all year 'round.

In July you may see "sundogs." These are short rainbows that appear on one or both sides of the sun sometimes before a storm. Jimmy's yellow coat probably gleams in the sun.

There are many missions in Navajo country. Alice seems to have mixed up the name of her favorite hymn.

It sounds as though she meant "Leaning on the Everlasting Arms." I feel sure that for Alice, as for most Navajos, English is a second language.

Some schools in Navajoland now have parents and other community members on school boards. This was not always so. Some are now teaching Navajo culture so that students may have a good foundation in the Navajo way as well as the white man's way. This is very important for youngsters as, when they have a good feeling about their heritage, they do better in other school subjects. Girls have always enjoyed an important place in Navajo culture and so Grandfather would be glad to have Alice do some of the things that the school may have planned just for boys.

Christmas is celebrated in most places and Alice has seen or been in plays about the birth of Jesus at Sunday School or maybe even in a school she has attended. There are Christmas parties, and candies and gifts are given to the children. Alice Yazzie gives tobacco to Grandfather, and her grandfather gives her a handmade silver bracelet with a setting of blue turquoise. Navajos are very famous for making silver jewelry, squash blossom necklaces, bracelets, rings, and many kinds of jewelry, often with the beautiful blue turquoise.

Alice Yazzie, like all Navajos, knows that Beauty is before her; Beauty is behind her; Beauty is below her; Beauty is above her; Beauty is all around her. And Beauty is Happiness.

Carl N. Gorman
Director of Navajo Resources
and Curriculum Development
Navajo Community College
Tsailie, Arizona

*This book is for Joy and Byron Harvey whose friendship
has been both hardy and perennial.—R.M.*

*I dedicate these visions to all the girls of the Navajo Nation who
embody the spirit of Alice Yazzie. Grow into your holiness, into your
lives. Sow and harvest compassion and strength. Hózhó. —S.B.*

Tricycle Press
a little division of Ten Speed Press
P.O. Box 7123
Berkeley, California 94707
www.tenspeed.com

The publisher would like to thank Gloria Grant of Rough Rock
Community School for her help with the new edition of this book.

BOOK DESIGN BY TASHA HALL
Typeset in Adobe Caslon

Library of Congress Cataloging-in-Publication Data
Maher, Ramona, 1934–1996
Alice Yazzie's year / by Ramona Maher ; illustrations by Shonto Begay.
p. cm.
Summary: Describes each month of a year in the life
of an eleven-year-old Navajo girl, Alice Yazzie, from
January, Yas Niłt'ees, to December, Nłch'itsoh.
ISBN 1-58246-080-9
1. Navajo Indians—Juvenile fiction. [1. Navajo Indians—Fiction.
2. Indians of North America—Southwest, New—Fiction.]
I. Begay, Shonto, ill. II. Title.
PZ7.M2764 Al 2003
[Fic]dc21
2002155292

First published by Coward, McCann & Geoghegan, Inc.
First Tricycle Press printing, 2003
Manufactured in China
1 2 3 4 5 6 — 07 06 05 04 03